Shapes of Australia

KU-039-289

Shapes of

Bronwyn

Australia

Bancroft

LITTLE HARE
www.littleharebooks.com

Treetops circle each other

in a wild bush dance.

Big boulders withstand

the fast-flowing creek.

Skyscrapers rise

like crystal shards.

Majestic mountains merge easily

with a long horizon.

Grasslands create

a quilt of nature's comfort.

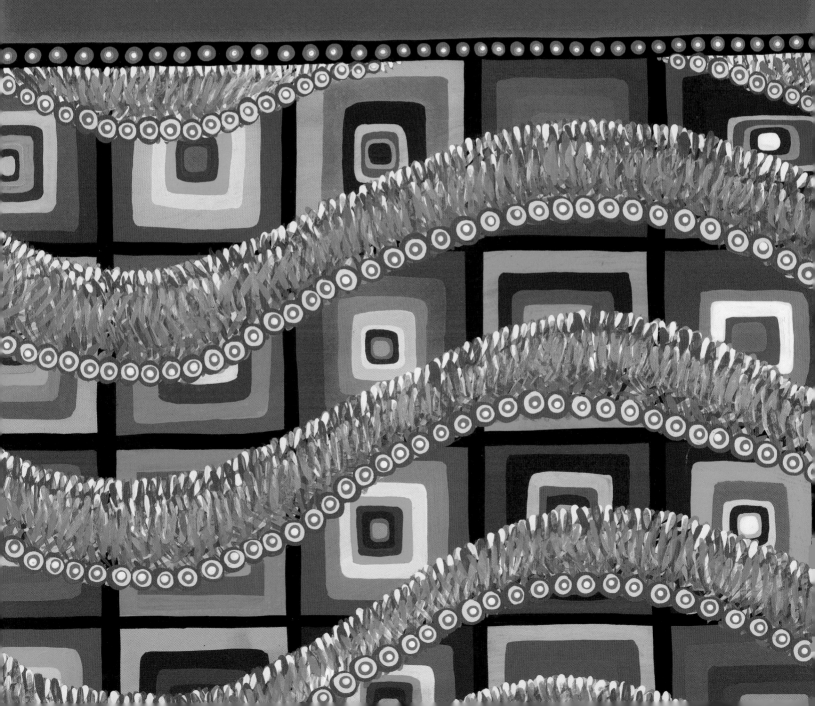

Termite nests settle comfortably

by a doomed tree.

The wavy sea frolics

around monsters of rock.

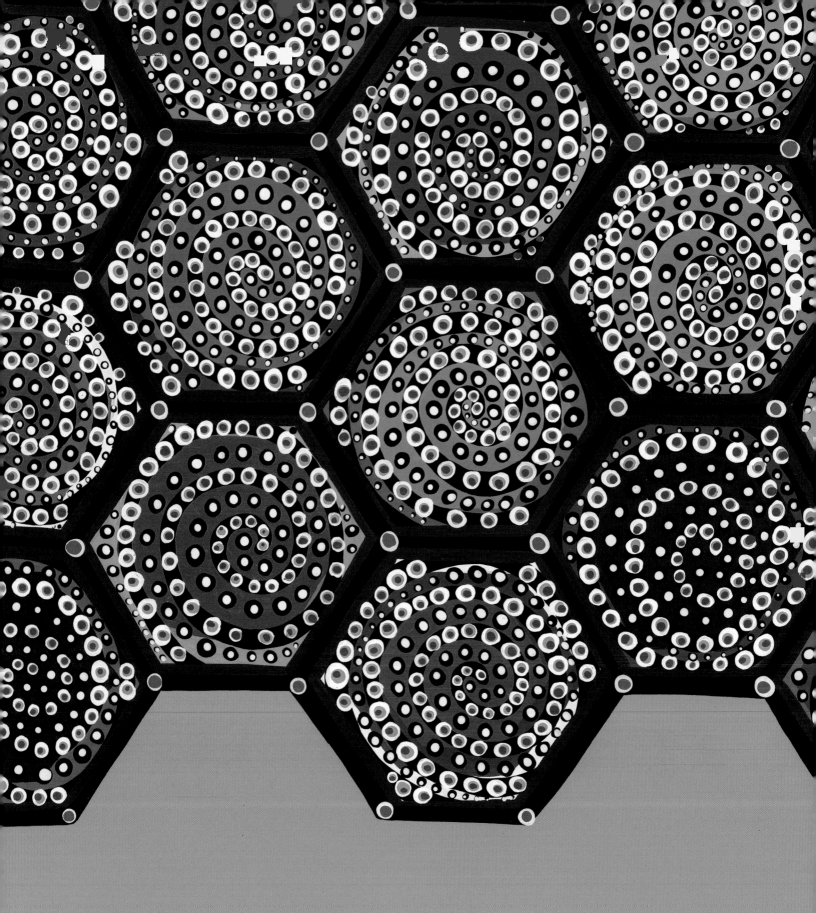

Native bees nurture their

honeycomb home.

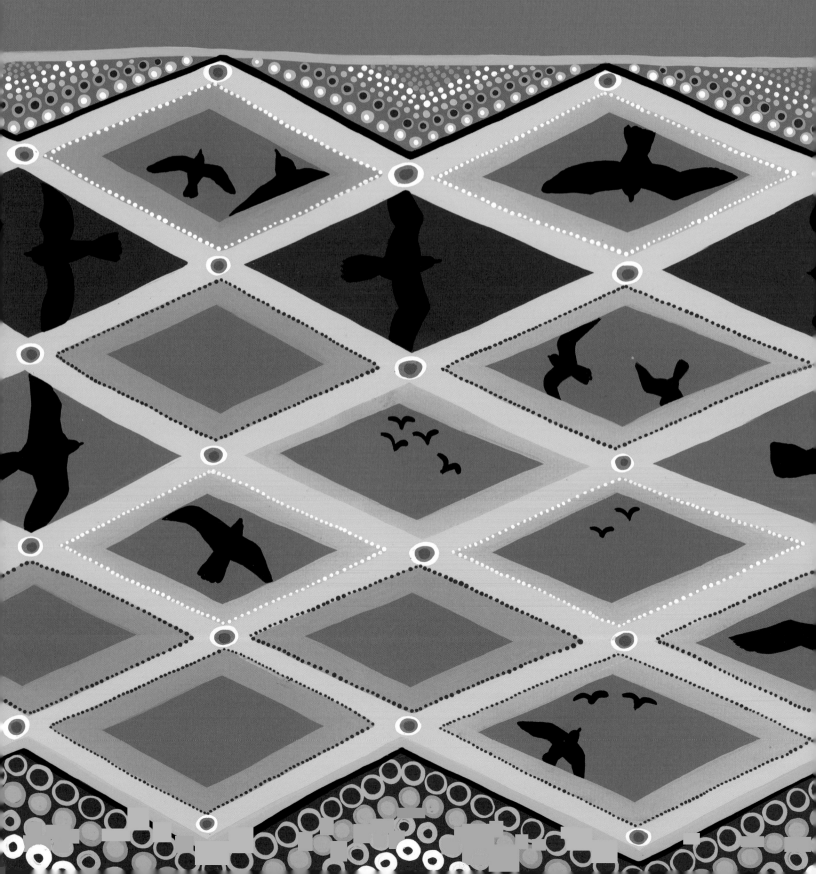

Birds fly an exhilarating trapeze

in the sky.

Mystical forms inhabit

the ocean floor.

I dedicate this book to the unique nature
and beauty of the Australian landscape.

Bronwyn Bancroft is a Djanbun clan member of the Bundjalung Nation.
In a career spanning over three decades, Bronwyn has participated in
hundreds of exhibitions, both solo and group, within Australia and overseas.

Collections that have acquired her work are: National Gallery of Australia,
Macquarie University, Art Gallery of New South Wales, Art Gallery of Western
Australia, State Library of New South Wales, State Library of Victoria,
Australian Museum and Artbank, as well as overseas collections such as
Newark Museum USA, Prime Minister of Turkey, The Kelton Foundation USA,
Volkerkunde Museum, Germany and Westpac USA.

Bronwyn has worked as a volunteer at Boomalli Aboriginal Artists
Co-operative for the last 8 years as curator, business planner and
senior strategist. Bronwyn currently holds Board positions with
Australian Indigenous Mentoring Experience (AIME), Boomalli
Aboriginal Artists Co-operative, Commonwealth Bank RAP Committee,
Arts Law and Copyright Agency.

Bronwyn has a Diploma of Visual Arts; two Masters degrees from the
University of Sydney, one in Studio Practice and the other in Visual Art;
and she is currently a Doctoral candidate at the University of Sydney.

Little Hare Books
an imprint of
Hardie Grant Egmont
Ground Floor, Building 1, 658 Church Street
Richmond, Victoria 3121, Australia
www.littleharebooks.com

Copyright © Bronwyn Bancroft 2017

First published 2017
First published in paperback 2017
Reprinted 2018, 2019 (twice)

All rights reserved. No part of this publication may be reproduced, stored in a retrieval
system or transmitted in any form or by any means, electronic, mechanical, photocopying,
recording or otherwise, without the prior written permission of the publisher.

Cataloguing-in-Publication details are available from the National Library of Australia
9781760501198 (pbk)

Edited by Margrete Lamond
Production management by Sally Davis
Designed by Vida & Luke Kelly
Produced by Pica Digital, Singapore
Printed through Asia Pacific Offset
Printed in Shenzhen, Guangdong Province, China

8 7 6 5 4

- -

The illustrations in this book were created using acrylic paints on archival paper.